# SUN & SON

amicus ink

Mankato, Minnesota

To my son Andy and grandsons Nikoli and Patrick—L.J.S.

For Freddie—R.S.

# SUN
# &
# SON

**WITHDRAWN**

written by **Linda Joy Singleton**

illustrated by **Richard Smythe**

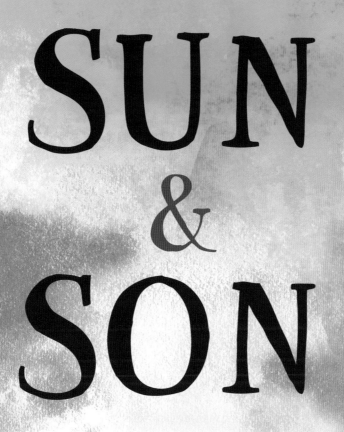

Rise.

Rise.

Shine.

Shine.

Grow.

Grow.

Warm.

Warm.

# Shadow.

Shadow.

Reflecting.

Reflecting.

Shimmer.

Shimmer.

Hide.

Hide.

Peek.

Peek.

Set.

Set.

Glow.

Glow.

# Beam.

Beam.

Together.

Text copyright © 2022 by Linda Joy Singleton

Illustrations copyright © 2022 by Richard Smythe

Edited by Rebecca Glaser

Art direction and design by Christine Vanderbeek

Published in 2022 by Amicus Ink, an imprint of Amicus
P.O. Box 227, Mankato, MN 56002 · www.amicuspublishing.us

### Library of Congress Cataloging-in-Publication Data

Names: Singleton, Linda Joy, author. | Smythe, Richard, 1986- illustrator. | Title: Sun & son / by Linda Joy Singleton; illustrated by Richard Smythe.
Other titles: Sun and son | Description: First edition. | Mankato, MN : Amicus Ink, imprint of Amicus, 2022. | Audience: Ages 4-8. | Summary: Told in
a sequence of verbs, the activities of a boy's day with his father mirror the sun's journey in the sky from rising in the morning to setting in the evening.
Identifiers: LCCN 2020026702 (print) | LCCN 2020026703 (ebook) | ISBN 9781681527475 (hardcover) | ISBN 9781681527482 (ebook) | Subjects:
CYAC: Fathers and sons--Fiction. | Sun--Fiction. | Classification: LCC PZ7.S6177 Su 2022 (print) | LCC PZ7.S6177 (ebook) | DDC [E]--dc23
LC record available at https://lccn.loc.gov/2020026702 | LC ebook record available at https://lccn.loc.gov/2020026703

First edition 9 8 7 6 5 4 3 2 1
Printed in China